MW01534530

MUSHING IS MURDER

COZY MYSTERY TAILS OF ALASKA, BOOK 1

PATTI BENNING

SUMMER PRESCOTT BOOKS PUBLISHING

Copyright 2019 Summer Prescott Books

All Rights Reserved. No part of this publication nor any of the information herein may be quoted from, nor reproduced, in any form, including but not limited to: printing, scanning, photocopying, or any other printed, digital, or audio formats, without prior express written consent of the copyright holder.

**This book is a work of fiction. Any similarities to persons, living or dead, places of business, or situations past or present, is completely unintentional.

The small airport was almost empty by the time people began disembarking the plane. Angie Seaver was used to the bustling hubbub of major international airports, and the difference was disconcerting.

The second disconcerting thing was how much older her father looked. She spotted him before he saw her, and stumbled to a halt so suddenly that her overly large suitcase almost knocked her over. The video chats hadn't shown just how tired he looked, or how the grey in his hair was almost white, or the deep lines around his eyes and mouth. It had been nearly ten years since she had seen him in person, and in those ten years, he had aged twenty.

A sudden feeling of guilt overwhelmed her, followed

quickly by resolve. She had made the right decision by coming here. She knew that now, more certainly than ever.

"Dad?"

Her father jerked as if he had fallen asleep leaning against the wall. He rubbed his eyes, then turned to look her up and down. The smile that grew on his face made her feel even worse for the rift of time that had come between them.

"Angie." He reached out and pulled her into a hug, heedless of her suitcase and bulky bags. "How was your flight?"

"Bumpy. And cramped. I'm glad it's over. How far is home from here?"

"About an hour," he said. He stepped back and looked at her again, as if he couldn't believe she was actually there. He shook his head, then reached out to grab her suitcase. "Come on, let's head out to the car. I've got an early day tomorrow."

Lost Bay, Alaska. Angie stared out of her window at the little town, simultaneously surprised at how it had changed and at how it hadn't. She had grown up here, and the layout of the streets was as familiar to her as her own apartment had been, but there were enough differences to throw her off occasionally. Mr. Bean's, the coffee shop, bore a permanent *Closed* sign in the window. On the corner, she spotted its replacement; Snow Grounds, which bore a logo of a stylized mug and a snow-covered mountain. Her family's diner, Lost Bay Burgers, was still there, as unchanged as the coast they had just driven along for the better part of an hour.

It was well past midnight by now, and the town was quiet. It could have been a ghost town. The fresh snowfall on the roads was unmarked by tire tracks, and she hadn't seen another living person since they had left the airport.

"Home sweet home," she murmured.

"What was that, Ange?" her father asked, glancing over at her.

"I was just thinking about how familiar this all looks."

He nodded. "It'll always be your home. You never really leave a place like this."

Angie remained silent at that. She wasn't sure her father was right. She had left, for ten years. Her

brother had left, and showed no sign of ever returning. And her sister... well, Angie didn't like to think
about her sister.

"How are the dogs?" she asked instead, changing the
subject to something she knew her dad was sure to
latch on to. Sure enough, a broad smile lit up
his face.

"The team's great this year. They're really promising.
We sold some dogs to Bill Grand a few years back —
do you remember him? — to bring in some new
blood. We still have Petunia, though. Remember
her? You used to love that dog. She's getting up there
now, but she still helps teach the new pups the rules
every year."

Angie smiled. She'd always loved her father's sled
dogs growing up. She had helped take care of them
when she was a child, and even when she got older
and got her first apartment in town, she had often
stopped by to feed and exercise the dogs.

"I wonder if she'll remember me," she mused.
Petunia was a red and white Alaskan husky, a mix of
a wide variety of breeds bred for the sole purpose of
endurance racing. Her dad owned both mixed breed
Alaskan huskies, and purebred Siberian huskies.

"What about Boots? He was in the same litter as her, wasn't he?"

Her father shook his head. "He was her half-brother, and he was a few years older than her. He lived to be sixteen. Not a bad age for a dog, if you think about it."

"Oh."

They fell silent after that. Angie knew her father's thoughts were on his old dogs. Hers were on the past. It was hard not to think of all of the happy years she'd had here when she was younger. There was a time when she swore she'd never leave this place. When she wanted to follow in her father's footsteps and raise sled dogs, giving rides to tourists in the summer and racing in the winter.

But all of that changed after her sister died. It broke their family as a whole, just as it broke each of their hearts. Her brother, who had already been drifting away, cut ties completely, not even coming to her funeral. Angie had stayed half a year longer, but eventually she just couldn't take it anymore and left, fleeing to the south where she could build new memories for herself in southern California. New memories and a new family, that had been the plan.

And now she was back, and it was almost like she hadn't left at all. She was older, but she didn't really feel any different. Nothing had changed here, or so it seemed. Not really.

Still, she remembered her father's tired face as he had stood waiting for her at the airport and knew that she had made the right decision. It was time to start making amends, before it was too late.

"We're almost there," her father said. Angie jolted. She had been so lost in her thoughts that she hadn't even noticed that they had left town and were now driving through the wilds of coastal Alaska. Occasional spots of light showed where someone's house was, but they were few and far between.

"Okay," she replied, gripping her purse more tightly on her lap at the swirl of nerves that made her stomach clench.

"Be quiet when we go in. Your mother's going to be asleep, and I don't want to wake her. Today was a bad day."

"Okay."

So she wouldn't see her mother tonight. Her

stomach twisted again, but this time with worry, not with nerves. Just how bad were things?

The car turned onto the familiar driveway. The trees were a little bigger and — by the feel of it — the ruts a little deeper, but other than that it could have been just yesterday that she had left. She sat forward in her seat, hungrily taking in the view of her child-hood home.

It was two stories tall, and had been made at a time when faux-log cabin homes were stylish. The house had a couple of sprawling additions, the guest bedroom and an extra bathroom, where she would be staying, and a workshop where her father crafted everything from sleds to wooden figurines.

The kennel was behind the house. She could see the chain link fencing that surrounded the dog yard from the car. That was a relatively new addition, one her father had been forced to add after someone had stolen three of his dogs and had unleashed a few others. She could hear the dogs barking, awakened by the sound of the truck coming up the drive.

It was home.

Her father parked in front of the house and grabbed

her suitcase from the back before heading up to the front door. She followed behind him, gathering her other bags into her arms and trying not to slip on the packed-down snow. It was *cold*. She had forgotten just how cold Alaska could get. It was the sort of cold that bit at her skin as if it had teeth and made her eyes water.

"There we go," her father said quietly, pushing open the front door. "The lock sticks sometimes, so you've got to wiggle it. Before I forget, here are the keys. I made a new set for you. I didn't know if you still had your own."

"Thanks, Dad." She managed to take the keys without dropping anything. Her father stood aside to let her into the house, shutting the door behind her. She breathed out a sigh of relief. It was nice and warm inside, and smelled just how she remembered it.

"Let's get your stuff in your room," he said.

She took a step forward, only to almost trip over a cat. It wound around her legs, purring. She spotted another feline face peering at her from the back of the couch. Both of them were black and white, almost identical from what she could see.

"Dad?"

"Yeah?"

"I thought you hated cats."

He glanced back at her, noting the cat on the floor and the one on the couch. His gruff gaze softened.

"The one by your feet is Checkers and the one on the couch is Chess. They're your mother's."

"I thought *Mom* hated cats. We never had any growing up."

"I guess things changed after you two left." He shrugged, looking fondly at the cat by her feet. "The house was quiet. Someone dumped these two off in the dumpster behind the old coffee shop. Bill's wife brought them in to the diner, only two weeks old and almost frozen to death. Your mom nursed them back to health, and they never left."

Angie smiled at the cats. Her hands were too full to pet them, and she was about to put down her stuff when her father started moving again, heading toward the guest room.

She followed him, one of the cats trailing along behind them. Her father stopped at the end of the hallway and opened a door, stepping back. A white and red bundle of fur came running out, skidding to a stop inches from Angie's legs.

"Petunia," she breathed, unable to help the smile that spread across her face.

The dog sniffed at her legs for a long moment. She could see the exact instant Petunia realized who she was. The dog's whole body seemed to wag as she spun around, an excited whine filling the hallway. Angie let her bags fall and crouched down to greet the dog.

"Hey, girl," she said, scratching the husky behind her ears. The dog was still wiggling, her tongue darting out in an effort to lick Angie's face. She felt another, sharper, sting of guilt. "I've been gone too long, I know. I'm sorry. I'm back now."

The dog broke loose of her grip and tackled her, joyfully snuffling Angie's clothing as the woman laughed. She looked up to see her father smiling at them.

"Thought you might want to see her. I know how you always used to like having the dogs sleep inside when you were little. She spends the cold nights in here anyway, now. There's a dog bed in your room if you want her to keep you company."

"Thank you, Dad," she said, meeting his eyes, trying to communicate everything that she couldn't say into her gaze. That she was sorry, that she had missed him and the dogs and her mother, that she was ready to fix all of the broken things that had torn their family apart.

He just nodded. "I'll leave you here, then. I'm taking the dogs out for an early run in the morning. I'll put the coffee pot on before I go out. Everything's the same in the kitchen. You'll be able to find stuff for breakfast?"

"I'll figure it out," she said. "What time does Mom usually wake up?"

"She could get up at four, or she could get up at ten. It varies. I let her sleep as long as possible when I can. I think she'll be up early, though. She's excited to see you, Ange."

"I know. I'm excited to see her too."

They said their goodnights and Angie dragged her bags the rest of the way into the room. Her room. It was decently sized, with a comfortable looking bed, a desk, and a small sitting area with a plush armchair in the corner by an old-fashioned wood burning fireplace. Still, it was smaller than her apartment had been, and she wasn't sure how she would adjust to living with her parents again. This wasn't exactly as she had envisioned her life going. Of course, she hadn't ever thought that her sister would die, or her mom would get sick, either.

We make do, she thought. *That's all we can do.*

She looked down at Petunia, who was busy sniffing her bags. The last time Angie had seen her, the husky had been only a couple of years old. Now, she was twelve — no, thirteen. Old, not ancient, but getting up there. She was greying, and Angie could see a certain stiffness in some of her movements.

She had raised Petunia practically from birth. Her dam hadn't produced enough milk for the litter, and Angie had volunteered to take a couple of pups to her apartment to bottle feed them, so her parents wouldn't have to do it all. One little red and white puppy had wormed her way into Angie's heart, and had ended up spending more time with her than back at her parents' house with the rest of the dogs. It had been heartbreaking to leave Petunia behind when she moved to California, but the dog loved doing what she had been bred for, and there weren't many dog sledding opportunities in the city.

"I'm back, girl," Angie said. "Not for good, but for a while. And I want to make the most of it."

2

Angie woke up to sunlight streaming in through the south facing window, and a warm body curled up against her back. She reached over and felt soft fur. Petunia, it seemed, had given up on the dog bed partway through the night.

She stretched and then reached for her cell phone, which was on the nightstand. It was just past eight. She still felt tired, thanks to the late night and hours spent traveling, but she knew there would be no getting back to sleep. Not with the tempting scent of a home-cooked breakfast wafting in from the hallway.

Her parents' house looked different in the light than it had in the dark. Now that it was daytime, she could see little changes here and there; a new set of china in the cabinet, a wall that had been stripped of wallpaper and painted a pale green, a stretch of new carpeting in the hallway, and a whole new set of furniture in the living room.

The kitchen was mostly unchanged, other than one glaring difference. Her mother. When Angie had last seen her mother, the other woman had just begun to go grey, and had died her roots religiously as if she could stave off the aging process through the use of artificial color. Now, she had a head of grey hair with only a few hints of auburn throughout. She had lost weight, too, and seemed to have shrunken in on herself. She had a walker near to where she stood at the counter, and even from the doorway, Angie could see the way her hands shook.

No one could have predicted that Angie's mother would develop Parkinson's disease, not at such a young age. It had progressed steadily over the years since it had been diagnosed, and Angie realized that her parents had hid the worst of it from her during their video calls. Seeing her mother like this was a shock. If Angie hadn't already decided that coming back was the right choice, the image of her mother standing at the counter, trying to pour two glasses of orange juice with shaking hands would have solidi-fied it for her.

"Hey, Mom," she said softly.

Her mother looked up, and a warm smile spread across her face. Angie closed the distance between them, and the two women enveloped each other in a hug.

"Angie. How did you sleep?" Her mother's voice was quiet, softer than Angie remembered.

"I slept well. How long have you been up? Is Dad still out with the dogs?"

Her mother nodded. "He won't be back in for another couple of hours. I've only been up since seven. I had a feeling you were going to get up soon. You've never been one to sleep in very late. I made breakfast for the two of us. The sausage is from the neighbors. Remember Cheryl and Dave? They're looking forward to seeing you again."

"I'll have to go over and say hi pretty soon. Breakfast smells great. Do you want me to set the table?"

"Sure, if you don't mind. You know where everything

is. We haven't moved anything around since you left."

Sure enough, Angie found everything where she had left it and got to work setting the kitchen table. She and her mother sat down together and ate slowly enough that they could converse between bites. They talked about their friends, work, movies they'd seen — everything but the tough topics like her sister's death and her mother's illness. Once Ange had finished with her plate, she got up and started doing the dishes while her mother fed the cats and Petunia.

"Oh, I almost forgot," her mother said as she came back into the kitchen. "Your father left this for you."

Angie took the folded piece of paper and opened it to find a handwritten note. *Ange, I left the keys to the diner in the center console of the old van. You can use the van while you're here if you want. If you can go open the diner by eight, that would be great. I'll stop by this afternoon to check on things. Love, Dad.*

She blinked, then re-read the note. A glance at the clock showed her that it was after nine already. "Shoot," she said. "I'm already late."

"What is it, sweetie?"

"Dad wants me to open the diner this morning. I know I came back to help out with the family business, but I wasn't expecting to be thrown in the deep end like this. I thought he'd show me the ropes, spend some time there with me while I get to know the other employees and get familiar with the kitchen again, that kind of stuff. I should have known better. This is so Dad. I was supposed to open it at eight, and he didn't even mention it last night."

"He doesn't mean anything by it, you know," her mother said. "He just has a lot of faith in you. It doesn't occur to him that it's been over a decade since you worked there, and you may not remember how to run the place. Do you want me to come with you this morning? I usually take a nap around noon, but I can put it off until later this evening. I don't want you to worry yourself over the diner if you don't have to."

"No... I'll figure it out." She stuffed the note in her pocket with a sigh. "I'm here to make things easier for you, Mom, not harder. I wish Dad had taken the time to actually sit down with me and talk about what I'm supposed to do there, but I'll figure it out. It's like riding a bike, right?"

Her confidence faded as she neared town in the rickety old van forty minutes later. The annoyance at her father was still seething inside her, all too familiar. *It's not like he was forced to take the dogs out this morning*, she thought. *He makes his own training schedule. It wouldn't have killed him to put off the run until this afternoon. Is it really too much to expect him to take an hour to show me the ropes at the diner? I have no idea what I'm doing. Even back when I worked there, I never managed the place.*

By the time she reached the gravel parking lot in the back of the diner, she felt ready to snap at the first person who said the wrong thing. Luckily, the place was empty when she got there. She used the key she found in the center console to unlock the diner's back door and let herself inside. The first thing that struck her was that it smelled exactly the same as she remembered. It even looked like nothing had changed. Even the register looked the same. It had gone from antique to dinosaur in the past decade. Her father was someone who rarely changed anything as long as it worked. He ate the same thing for breakfast almost every day, he never replaced a vehicle until it literally fell apart around him, and he wore the same outfits he had since she was a child. The dogs and the sport he loved were the only things he stayed up to date on, and she had no doubt that the sled he was using right at this very moment was a cutting edge piece of technology, and was probably made out of materials that were decades more modern than the cash register.

Grumbling to herself, Angie found the light switch and flicked it on, then looked around to get a feel for the state of the place. It was old, yes, but at least it was clean. Whoever had closed up the night before had done a good job of making sure everything was ready for the next day. Without tables to clean or napkin holders to refill, Angie found herself at a loss. What exactly did opening the diner entail? Was she supposed to start cooking? Weren't there supposed to be other employees, for that matter?

Feeling a bit lost, Angie went over to the front doors and unlocked them, then headed toward the kitchen. She was relieved to see a printed-out schedule taped to the wall. *Tuesday: Rod Seaver and Grace Bishop: 8 — 3. Betty Johnson and Theodore Wiggin 3-9.*

That left the question of where this Grace person was. It was nearly ten, almost two hours since the diner was supposed to open and no one had called the landline, and Angie hadn't seen any other cars in the parking lot. Had the employee shown up and decided to take the day off when she found the doors closed and locked and no one there to open them? She didn't know, and since she couldn't find any phone numbers for the employees, she didn't have a way to find out.

"Guess I'm on my own," she muttered. "If Dad doesn't like how I do things, that's his own fault."

She decided to start the day by making coffee. Coffee, she figured, was a staple in any diner, and at least the coffee makers weren't something she needed instructions for. She made a pot of regular and a pot of decaf, and while the coffee makers were gurgling away, she snagged a menu from behind the front counter and began reading through the options.

It didn't seem like there were any major changes here, either, but at least the menus themselves had been replaced. She didn't find any surprises, and was confident that she could make anything the menu listed. Eggs, hash browns, burgers, fries... she'd spent a few years working here during and after high school, and even though it had been a while, she could probably make any of those in her sleep.

By the time the coffee was done, there was still no sign of any customers, so she took the opportunity to familiarize herself with the kitchen. Cheese, milk, and eggs in the fridge, meat in the freezer, pancake mix and buns in the cupboard. There was a shake and malt machine that *was* new, and she didn't want to try to figure that out without instructions, and a soda machine that she was pretty sure was as old as she was.

All in all, Angie felt surprisingly comfortable in the diner despite her initial fears. It was all coming back to her, with a strange sense of deja vu. She found an old employee handbook and began reading through it, getting so lost in the list of rules that she almost missed it when the bell over the front door jingled. Her first customer.

He had already taken a seat at the counter by the time she came out of the kitchen. He was an older man, about her father's age or maybe a few years older. She didn't recognize him, but she wasn't surprised when a broad grin lit up his face as he laid eyes on her.

"Little Angie Seaver!" he exclaimed. "Rod told me you'd be coming back to work here soon. How long you been here?"

"I flew in last night," she said.

"You're jumping in feet first, eh?"

She gave him a tight smile. "Yeah, you could say that."

"Your dad out running the dogs?"

"You know him well, Mr..."

"Hal O'Brien," he said, shaking her hand enthusiastically. "You went to school with my Mags."

"Oh, Mr. O'Brien. Sorry I didn't recognize you. How are you? How's Maggie?" No wonder he was so familiar. Maggie had been her best friend growing up. Her father, who had worked as a police officer at the time, had been a vague figure on the outskirts of Angie's life for as long as she could remember.

"It's all right, I know I've gained a few pounds and lost a few hairs." He chuckled. "I'm doing all right.

Mags is doing as well as could be expected. Her husband ran out on her, and she's back to living in town with the little tyke, Joshua. He's nine now, just had his birthday last month. You should give her a call sometime. I got her a job at the police station, so she's doing all right."

"I will," Angie promised. "There are a lot of people I need to get in touch with. So, what can I get you today, Mr. O'Brien?"

"Give me a plate of extra cheesy scrambled eggs, three strips of bacon, and a toasted English muffin with some of that jam your mom makes. And keep my coffee cup filled up, I'm going to need the energy today."

She reached for her notepad, only to realize she had forgotten it in the kitchen. With a sigh, she tried to commit the order to memory, something that had never been a skill of hers.

"The coffee's coming right out, and I'll get everything else started," she said. "It was nice to see you again, Mr. O'Brien."

"You too, Angie. I'll tell Mags to give you a call. The two of you should catch up."

She shot him a smile, then hurried back into the kitchen, already feeling in over her depth. What had the order been again? Scrambled eggs with extra cheese, bacon... toast? And what flavor of jam had he wanted? She knew there had been a couple of different flavors in the fridge.

Taking a deep breath, Angie poured coffee into a mug and took it out to him, then got to work on the rest of the meal.

3

By the time one of her father's employees showed up, Angie had already made three mistakes on orders, had received five complaints that the food didn't taste "the same," and had spilled a mug of decaf coffee on herself. When she heard the restaurant's back door open and turned to see a familiar face, she almost melted in relief.

"Mrs. Johnson," she said, approaching the older woman. "Thank goodness you're here! I have no idea what I'm doing."

"We'll talk business soon, but first, I need to hug my little angel."

Angie found herself pulled into a hug, surrounded

by the familiar strong arms and flowery scent of the woman she had known all her life. Betty Johnson had been at the diner since the beginning, and had been a fixture in Angie's childhood. She remembered long, lazy summers spent at the diner, helping wait tables and clean dishes under the strict but caring eye of the older woman.

Betty pulled back after a moment and looked Angie up and down, giving a *tsk* of disapproval. "Look how skinny you are. Is your father not feeding you enough?"

"I just got here yesterday," Angie told her. "And don't worry, I'm sure I'll gain plenty of weight working here. You know how weak I am around deep-fried mushrooms."

"Well, good. You need some meat on your bones. Now, what's going on?"

She took a deep breath. "Dad didn't tell me I was supposed to open at eight, and I didn't get here until almost ten, and the other employee never showed up. Then I messed up Mr. O'Brien's order and I don't know how my dad cooks stuff so everything tastes different than people are used to, and to cap it all off I spilled coffee on myself and smell like I should be working in a coffee shop."

"Wow, you've had quite the day, haven't you? Let's start from the beginning. Who else was supposed to be here?"

"Someone named Grace. I don't know her, or at least, I don't think I do."

Betty shook her head. "You wouldn't. She only started working here two years ago. Did you check the answering machine?"

Angie stared at the older woman. "Answering machine?"

Betty led the way over to the counter, where a sleek black landline was sitting in a cradle. There was a blinking light on top. "The old phone saw its last days a couple years ago, and your dad finally upgraded it. Here, you just press the button next to the speaker to hear the messages." She pressed it, and a woman started speaking.

"Hey, it's Grace. My dentist appointment got moved up to nine, so I'm not going to be able to come in at all today. Umm... I'll try your cell phone, I guess, Mr. Seaver. Sorry about this, but I don't want to reschedule again. If I do, I'll just be thinking about it the whole time. Who knew getting your wisdom teeth out could be so terrifying?" There was the sound of nervous laughter. "So, I'll be in on Saturday I guess, if everything goes well. Thanks for the time off, and I'll pick up an extra shift next week or something to make up for this. Um, I think that's it. Bye!"

The message ended. Angie shook her head. "I feel pretty dumb right now. I can't believe I didn't see that. I wonder if she ever got in touch with my dad."

"Has he stopped in yet?"

"Not yet. He's supposed to come by sometime this afternoon."

"Then he'll probably be here soon. Come on, let's get this place ship shape. I have a box of sweaters I was going to donate to my church in the car. You go pick one out and soak your shirt so that the coffee doesn't stain it. I'll go handle the customers while you get situated, then I'll come back here and answer any questions you have."

"Thanks," Angie said. "You're a lifesaver."

With Betty's help, things went much more smoothly. Being in a clean shirt helped Angie feel more like herself, and having someone to ask when one of the customers ordered something that wasn't on the menu helped a lot. Most of the guests were regulars, and they each had their favorite dishes and particular ways they wanted things cooked. A good half of them recognized Angie, and the going was slow whenever one of them spotted her for the first time. The older woman was a lifesaver — without her, there was no telling how much food Angie would have burned.

When her father came in shortly before four, he wasn't alone. His old friend Bill Barkly was at his side, and they were both chuckling at a joke when they came through the door.

"Angie!" Bill cried when he saw her. "Rod said you were here, but I told him I wouldn't believe it until I saw you with my own eyes. How's your first day back been?"

As he spoke, he and her father took seats at the counter. Her father gave her a nod, which she returned.

"It's been going about as well as could be expected," she said. "Thank goodness for Betty. She's been a lifesaver. I hardly remember anything from the last time I worked here."

She shot a glance at her father, wondering if he would apologize for leaving her in the lurch like he had. He just nodded. "Betty's great. I don't know what I'd do without her. If she ever starts talking about retiring, I'm going to have to offer to double her salary to keep her."

"She makes the best brisket, too," Bill said appreciatively. "Remember Christmas Eve? I ate so much here that I hardly had room for Christmas dinner the next day. If you added her brisket to the menu permanently, you would be a millionaire by this time next year. The whole state would travel to Lost Bay just to eat it."

"I've raised the idea with her before," her father said. "She's insistent that the brisket is for holidays only. I doubt she even makes it for her husband other than on holidays."

Seeing that the conversation had gotten permanently off track, Angie cleared her throat. "So, how are you doing, Bill?"

"Not bad, not bad," he said. "I'm retired and

enjoying life. It's nice to have the time to devote to the dogs. I'm finally able to hit all the races I want to, not that it's paying off. My dogs did horribly in the last race. Poor things just didn't have any heart. If I didn't know better, I'd say someone drugged them."

"And I told you, that's ridiculous, Bill. Dogs just have bad days sometimes, that's all," her father said.

Angie decided to cut off the argument before it started and cleared her throat. "What can I get you two? Coffee?"

Both men nodded. "And bring out the good creamer," Bill said. "I'll take a cheeseburger, no pickles, and can you caramelize the onions? I'd better take one of your BLTs back for my wife, too. Toasted, wheat bread, mayo on the side."

"Got it," Angie said, scribbling in her notepad. "Dad?"

"I'll take a chicken salad sandwich on toasted white bread, with the kettle cooked potato chips on the side. Could you make a fresh batch? I like them warm."

"All right. I'll see if I can get Betty to bring out your

coffee, since she'll love to hear you gossiping about her beef brisket, and I'll get the food started."

Angie was actually proud of herself for the burger she made Bill. She'd taken most of the afternoon to get the meat's time on the grill right, but she seemed to have nailed it at last with a perfect medium-well done burger. Betty walked her through making a batch of chicken salad, then sliced the potatoes for the kettle cooked chips.

When she dropped the food off for her father and Bill, she felt like a young child again, waiting for his approval, even though she had only made half the food. Bill took a bite of the burger and gave her a thumbs up.

"Just how I like it," he said. "Rod, I'm going to say your restaurant is in good hands."

"I never had any doubt," her father said. "Ange, if you want, you can head home now. I'll spend a few hours here, then I'm going to stop at the store and get stuff for dinner. Let your mother know that we'll be eating late, and Dave and Cheryl will be coming over. They're excited to see you."

"All right, if you're sure you don't need me here. Do you need me to do anything at home?"

"Just help your mother with the housework, if you can. You okay with opening most mornings? If so, I'll just put you on the morning shift for this week."

"Sure," she said. "I'll go tell Betty I'm leaving. I'll see you later, Dad."

4

The sun was already going down when Angie left the restaurant and headed home that evening. It had been a long day, and even though it was only just past five in the evening, she was exhausted. She wished she had thought to ask her father just how late the late dinner was going to be. She needed to catch up on sleep if she was going to be waking up early enough to open the diner at eight every day.

Despite her tiredness and the rough start, it had turned out to be a pretty good day. It was nice to see all of the people she had grown up with again, and once Betty was there to help her figure things out at the diner, the workday had gone smoothly. She had no doubt that before long working there would become second nature again.

She pulled up the long driveway and parked the car, getting out to the usual loud cacophony of dogs barking from the dog yard. She opened the front door — which her parents kept unlocked during the day when someone was home — and stooped to pet one of the cats. She wasn't sure whether it was Chess or Checkers. The sound of a laugh track on TV told her that her mother was in the living room.

Making her way to her bedroom, she dropped her purse on the armchair and collapsed on the bed. Thoughts of everything she had left behind in California flooded her mind. She had friends there, no one she was really close to, but people she would miss, nonetheless. An ex-boyfriend with whom things had been on the mend with, and a somewhat decent job in real estate that felt like it was actually going somewhere, but in the end neither had been *that* important to her. Not important enough to keep her from leaving.

It hadn't been easy to leave like she had, but it had felt inevitable. What had the alternative been? She could have said no, but then if something happened — if her mother got to the point where she needed constant help, if her father got hurt and couldn't run the diner anymore— she would have blamed herself. Her biggest fear was to live a life of regret, to look back on things she had done, or things she *should* have done, and have no way to fix her mistakes.

And so she had uprooted her life and moved to the frozen north. She could stay in touch with her friends, there would be other men that she liked, and at the end of the day her family was more important to her than a flashy job and an apartment with a rooftop pool.

But that didn't mean that she couldn't miss those things anyway.

Her bed dipped slightly as a cat jumped up on it. The cat sniffed her knee for a moment, then rubbed his face against it, purring. Angie stroked the feline's soft fur.

"I really need to learn to tell you two apart," she murmured. "Thanks, kitty. I'm feeling a bit better. Shall we go see if Mom needs any help? That's what I'm here for, after all."

She rose to her feet, feeling the soreness in her legs that came from standing all day. She felt a sudden pang for her office, with its plush leather swivel chair she practically sank into, then shook her head. She would get used to being on her feet all day. If someone Betty's age could do it, she sure could.

Her mother was in the living room, watching a re-run of an old sitcom. She looked up when Angie came in and smiled.

"How was your first day?" she asked in her soft voice.

"It went about as well as it could have," Angie said, taking a seat on the couch next to her mother. "It was nice to see all the familiar faces. How was your day?"

"It wasn't too bad. I didn't get as much done as I wanted to." The older woman sighed. "Did your father say what time he'd be home?"

"He was at the diner when I left and said he was going to stick around there for a while, then go to the store for food. He mentioned something about having a late dinner and inviting the neighbors."

Her mother nodded. "I talked to Cheryl on the phone, and she and Dave will be over here at about seven-thirty."

"All right. What needs to be done before then? I'm happy to help."

"The table needs to be set, and the wine needs to be brought up from the basement. The stairs are hard for me, and so is carrying the plates. Would you mind doing that?"

"Not at all." Angie got up. "Where's Pet? I wouldn't mind having her around while I help get everything ready."

"She's probably out with the other dogs. Your father took her out when he got back this morning to feed her and give her some time outside. She gets restless if she's in the house all day."

"I'll go grab her, then I'll get started on the table. Let me know if I can do anything else."

She retraced her steps to the front door and pulled on her boots and a parka she found in the closet before stepping outside. There was a well-worn path through the snow that led to the dog yard which she followed, keeping her fingers tucked into her coat pockets and her head down against the wind. She paused at the gate to enter the code on the padlock, then let herself into the fenced in yard. Looking up, she saw her father's team.

There were over twenty dogs in all, each of them tethered to a warm dog house with a platform on top. Most of them were watching her, some barking, some jumping excitedly against their tethers and wagging their tails. Most of them were dogs she didn't recognize, which wasn't surprising considering how long she'd been gone.

She had been apart from the mushing community for long enough that she could see how the set up might look to outside eyes. Someone who wasn't familiar with keeping dogs this way might see twenty dogs tied up to chains, living their lives outside in weather that was far too cold for a human and feel bad for them, but she knew that the dogs were well cared for and happy. The dog houses, which were raised off the ground and insulated with straw, kept the dogs warm even in the coldest of weather, and the tether gave them much more space to move around in than a kennel did. Even though most of the dogs got along with each other, it wouldn't have been safe to have twenty dogs running loose in even a big yard for long periods of time without supervision. Keeping them separate like this kept them safe.

Even though she liked having Petunia in the house with her, she understood why most of the dogs had to live outside. Any dog that lived inside wouldn't be acclimated to the cold, and wouldn't have as thick of a coat or as tough of paws as the dogs who were used to the weather. Dogs that weren't used to the weather could get cold or injured when they were out racing in the depths of an Alaskan winter. And there was no doubt that the dogs loved what they did. It was undeniable when she saw the excitement in the dogs' eyes when the harnesses came out, or when they saw a team straining against the sled before the snub line was released. They were happiest doing what they had been born and bred for; running.

It was addictive to humans too. Seeing the team like this made her itch to get back on the runners of a dog sled for the first time in ten years. It was an incomparable feeling, like flying through the snow. She never felt as connected to the dogs as she did when she was out mushing with a team.

But dogs, like humans, got older. According to her

father, Petunia still went on short runs to help with training the younger dogs, but she was retired from the racing team. She got sore, and at night, if she was outside, she got cold. After years of running at the lead of his team, she had earned a lazy retirement in front of the fireplace, and it seemed that she knew it.

"Hey, girl," Angie said as she approached the red and white husky. Petunia's whole body was wriggling as she approached, and she dropped down to roll around in the snow before bouncing up when Angie reached for the clasp that attached the chain to her collar. "Let's go inside."

The older dog knew the routine well, and dashed to the gate, waiting impatiently for it to be opened. Angie pushed it open and stepped out with the dog, pausing to redo the lock behind her. By the time she turned around, Petunia was already halfway down the worn path back to the house. Angie followed more slowly, watching as the dog paused by the building where the sleds were kept. She paused, looking back at Angie as if asking a question.

"No, sorry girl. We're just going inside." She gestured toward the house.

The dog ducked her head to grab a mouthful of

snow, then trotted the rest of the way up to the porch. Angie could see the stiff way she moved, but despite her age, the dog seemed just as happy as ever. *If humans were as positive as dogs*, she thought, *then the world would be a much better place.*

5

It was well past dark by the time dinner began. The five of them sat around the dining room table, Angie sitting in awkward silence while the older couples laughed about something she hadn't been around for. She liked Cheryl and Dave, but hadn't spent much time around them since her sister's funeral. She wasn't sure where the conversation would lead once they turned their attention to her, and would rather avoid the serious topics if she could.

"We're being rude, Dave," Cheryl said at last, touching her husband's arm. "You'll see Rod tomorrow, you can tell him your story about the bear then." She turned to Angie. "Now, Angie, dear, how are you doing? I was so thrilled when your mother told me you were coming back, but of course this has got to be quite a big change for you."

"I'm doing well," she replied, giving the older woman a smile. "It is a change, but it's really not as much of a change as I was expecting. Even after all this time, it's almost like I never left. Pretty much everything's the same here, which makes it a lot easier to adjust. How have you two been?"

"We're hanging in there," Cheryl said, her hand still on Dave's arm. "The winters are getting harder, of course. It used to be that I never thought twice about waking up in the dark to go feed the animals, but now my old bones start complaining the second my alarm goes off. Dave, of course, needs just as little sleep as always. He's out goodness knows how late at work, then gets up before I do in the morning."

Dave chuckled. "You forget that I take a nap in the middle of the day when I can."

"Maybe once a week," Cheryl scoffed. "You and those dogs of yours. You spend every spare second you have off practicing with Bill and Rod. You've got dog fur on the brain, Dave, I swear. The three of you are going out again tomorrow morning, leaving me to tend to everything else on my own."

"It's not fair to the dogs if they don't get their exercise," Dave said innocently. "It's too bad Angie's all grown up now. Remember when she was ten and she would come over before school every morning to feed the animals for us? I'm guessing two dollars a day wouldn't do it anymore."

Angie chuckled. She remembered her mother shaking her awake an hour before her siblings had to get up, making her keep good on her promise to the neighbors to work for them for the winter. It hadn't been a fun year, but the money *had* been nice back then.

"Sorry, my dad's already got me working my fingers to the bone at the diner."

"We'll have to stop in sometime and see you at work." Cheryl looked at Angie's mother and smiled. "You must be so proud of her, your little girl all grown up."

"I am," her mother said, but her smile didn't quite reach her eyes. Angie saw the sadness there, and knew she was thinking of her little girl who didn't get to grow up. The table fell silent as if everyone else's thoughts had gone to the same place. Cutting herself a small bite of salmon, Angie thought, *This. This is why I left.*

The next morning got off to a better start than the previous one had. She made it to the diner on time to open, and she met one of the employees she would be working with frequently, a teenager just out of high school named Theodore Wiggin, who told her everyone called him Theo.

He seemed to know his way around the diner better than she did, so she let him take care of the opening routine while she got the coffee started and prepared the waffle maker and the electric skillet for pancakes. She knew that at some point she would be taking over the managerial side of things, which had been her mother's job, but she needed to get familiar with how the place was run first.

"Excuse me, um, Mrs. Seaver?"

She looked up to see Theo standing next to her, looking nervous.

"You can call me Angie, if you want," she said. "I'm not married, plus whenever someone says Mrs. Seaver, I just think they're talking to my mother."

"All right, then. If you're sure. Angie... um, is that supposed to be waffle batter?"

She looked down at the bowl of batter she was mixing. "Yeah. Did I do something wrong?"

"Just... did you use the pancake mix to make it?"

"Was I not supposed to?"

He shook his head, still looking nervous, as if he was afraid he was going to get in trouble for correcting her. "We use the Belgian waffle mix in the pantry. The pancake mix sticks in the waffle maker, and it doesn't get that nice, crisp golden color that the Belgian mix does."

She sighed and looked down at the bowl. "Thanks for telling me, Theo. I still have a lot to learn."

The rest of the morning went surprisingly smoothly. She quickly got into the swing of things, making hash browns, eggs, and pancakes as if it was what she had spent the last ten years of her life doing. They were just about to switch over to their lunch menu when Theo came into the kitchen to get her.

"There's a guy out front that wants to see you, Miss

— Angie. Well, he wanted to see your dad, but I told him he's not here and he said you would do."

"Do you know who it is?" she asked.

"No. It's a regular, but I don't remember his name. Starts with an 'M' I think. He's more your age than Mr. Seaver's."

"All right," Angie said, her interest piqued. "Can you finish this omelet for me?"

Theo nodded. She washed her hands quickly, then went out into the dining area to find a handsome man who looked to be about her own age, give or take a year or two, waiting next to the register. His brown hair had snow and ice in it, and he was wearing thick gloves.

"Hi, I'm Angie Seaver," she introduced herself. "My employee said you wanted to speak with me?"

He shook her hand. "Malcolm Miles," he said. "I'm sorry to bother you at work, but I need to find your dad. I tried calling the house and no one picked up. I already know he isn't here, but I was hoping you'd know where to find him."

"I think he was planning on taking the dogs out and

running the team on our neighbors' property," she said, thinking back to the conversation from the night before. "I could try calling their number if you wanted. Cheryl might pick up."

He shook his head. "No, I just came from there. No one answered the door."

Angie frowned, beginning to feel concern. "What's going on?"

"I own the property bordering Cheryl and Dave's land. I was outside about an hour ago when a team of dogs came running across a field and came right up to my house. I managed to grab them. The sled was empty. There was no driver."

Angie's eyes widened. "The team lost their driver?" There was a certain amount of risk whenever anyone took a team of sled dogs out. Even people who had lived and breathed the sport for years sometimes made mistakes, and one slip or one too-sharp turn could send the driver flying off the sled. It wasn't unusual for the team to keep going if that happened, either unaware that they had lost their person, or spooked by the accident.

"Whose team was it?" she asked, her heart beginning to pound as visions of her father lying injured out in the snow somewhere flooded her mind.

"I don't know. I assumed it was Dave's, which is why I came to see if your dad could help me go look for him, but if your father was out there too…"

"You went to my family's house? My mom didn't answer the door?"

He shook his head. "We need to get out there and see if we can find the guy who's missing his team," he said. "The dogs are safe enough — I took them out of their harnesses and put them in my garage with some blankets — but whoever was on that sled might not be so lucky. I'd go on my own, but I don't know the local trails and I'd have no clue where to start."

She nodded. "I'll come help you figure out what's going on. Just give me a moment to tell my employee what's going on and see if I can make arrangements for someone else to come in. Dave and Cheryl have a lot of property. This could take a long time."

Consumed with worry, Angie followed Malcolm to Cheryl and Dave's house after arranging for things at the diner. While she was driving, she called the landline at her parents' house, and when that didn't work, she called her mother's cell phone.

"Hello?"

She felt a rush of relief when she heard her mother answer.

"Mom, where are you? Is everything okay?"

"Cheryl took me into town for some shopping and to get lunch," she said. "Why? What's going on?"

"Apparently the guy who lives on the other side of Dave and Cheryl found a team of dogs attached to a sled, but no driver. He couldn't find anyone at either house, so he came into town hoping to find Dad at the diner. He found me instead. I'm going to go help him search for whoever owns that sled. I'm guessing it's either Dad or Dave."

She heard her mom say something to someone else. "Cheryl says Bill was supposed to go out there with them too. We're on our way back. Oh dear, I hope no one's hurt."

Angie swallowed. "I hope so too, Mom."

She was surprised when instead of turning into Dave and Cheryl's driveway, Malcolm went a mile further down the road and turned onto what she assumed was his driveway. She hesitated at the turn off to Dave's, but decided to follow him instead.

"What are we doing here?" she asked as they got out of their cars. She could hear dogs barking, a sound that was so familiar that she hardly paid attention to it anymore.

"I figured we could grab my snowmobiles. It'll be faster than walking, and they're more maneuverable than a dog sled. Plus, if we find someone injured, we can carry them back more easily this way. Do you know how to drive one?"

"Of course."

He nodded. "Help me get them ready. We'll follow the trail the dogs left, and see if we can figure out what happened."

She got to work helping him, trying to ignore the sour feeling in her stomach. They were already on their way when it occurred to her that she should have asked to see the sled and the dogs. She might have been able to tell whether they were her father's, or someone else's. It would have been worth the extra few minutes to put her heart at ease.

The dogs had run a curving trail, driverless, through the field that bordered Dave and Cheryl's property. She could see where the uncontrolled sled had slammed into rocks and logs, likely scaring the dogs even further. It was pure luck that they had run in the direction of Malcolm's house, and that he had been able to grab the team as they ran by. They could have gone on for miles otherwise.

The going was slow as they picked their way through the field, but they sped up as they hit one of the groomed trails on Dave and Cheryl's property. There were old tracks from previous days, but luckily it had snowed during the night and the most recent ones were easy enough to pick out, even from the seat of a snowmobile.

She let Malcolm lead, following him almost on autopilot, as she looked around for any sign of the injured driver that he might have missed. If someone was calling for help, it would be almost impossible to hear them over the roar of the engines. She was about to signal to Malcolm to pull over so she could suggest that they stop every few minutes to cut the engines and listen for shouting when he pulled to a stop anyway.

He waved to get her to stop, but she was already slowing down. By the time she got her snowmobile stopped and the engine turned off, he was wading through the snow, across the 'Y' where two of the trails intersected. She saw what he was heading for before he reached it. A man was laying in the snow, and he wasn't moving.

6

"Bill," she breathed when she saw his face. She was ashamed at the rush of relief she felt that it wasn't her father. The feeling only lasted for a moment as Malcolm knelt down next to him and took off one of his gloves, touching his fingers to the unmoving man's cheek.

"He's cold," he said. "I don't think he's breathing."

Angie felt her stomach drop. "Can you find a pulse?"

Malcolm felt for it, then shook his head. "I don't think we made it on time," he said softly.

She moved forward to kneel beside him. Bill's eyes were open, and one of them was bloodshot. She reached out, then hesitated, not sure what she should do. Her eyes flicked to his hood, where she saw a drop of blood. Carefully, she pushed it back, revealing a bloody wound on his temple.

"He must have fallen off and hit a rock or something," she said. She felt numb, and not from the cold. She didn't know what to do in a situation like this. They both had their cell phones, but there wasn't any service this far out. They would have to leave him to go back to a house and call the police. And that still left the question of where her father and Dave were. Had something happened to them too? Were they still on the trails, unaware that one of their friends had been in a horrible accident?

She was suddenly reminded of the accident that had taken her sister's life, and the horror that had risen up in her when she realized she had spent hours living her own life, unaware that her younger sister was gone. It hadn't even felt real when she got the call. She hadn't wanted to believe that life could be so unfair. A phone call at the wrong time, a moment of distraction on an icy road, a tree in the wrong place, and everything had changed for all of them.

She shook the memories away. "You should stay here with him. I can take the snowmobile to Dave and

Cheryl's house and use their phone to call the police."

"Will you be able to get in? No one was there when I checked."

"I used to do odd jobs for them when I was a kid," she said. "I'm hoping they still keep their spare key in the same place. They probably do, nothing else seems to have changed in this town while I was gone."

He raised an eyebrow, but didn't comment on that. Instead, he just nodded. "Go," he said. "And hurry."

She pushed the snowmobile Malcolm had lent her to its limit as she followed the trails back toward David and Cheryl's house, slowing only as she rounded corners so as not to risk running headlong into a sled team if someone else was out on the trails.

She eased up a bit as the house came into view, and was turning the snowmobile toward the back porch when something caught her eye.

A man was standing by the tall pole barn, unhooking a team of dogs from his sled.

She hesitated, then changed direction, coming to a halt just feet away from Dave and his team. He was looking at her with a frown on his face, positioning himself so he was between her and his dogs. Belatedly, she realized he had no way to recognize her with all of the outdoor gear and the helmet she was wearing. She took the helmet off and cut the engine.

"Angie," he said. "What are you —"

"Bill's dead," she said, cutting him off. She winced as soon as the words were out of her mouth, realizing how blunt she had been. The adrenaline that was still pounding through her made it hard to think clearly. "I need a phone. We need to call the police."

Dave's eyes widened as she spoke. "Wait, slow down. What happened to Bill? Why are you even out here? I thought your dad said you were working today."

"It's a long story," she said. "But to keep it short, someone found Bill's team running loose with an empty sled and came around the diner looking for help, since he couldn't find anyone at my house or your house. We took his snowmobiles out to look for Bill and found him on one of the trails. It looks like he hit his head on something."

"There's a phone in the barn, to the right of the door. Just let me finish getting the dogs unhooked, and I'll join you." He shook his head. "Bill... I can't believe it. With what happened to your dad, and me running face first into a branch, I thought that was our bad luck for the day." He touched the beginnings of a bruise over his eye.

Angie took a step toward the door that led into the pole barn then paused, turning back around. "Wait, what happened to my dad?"

"One of his lines broke and a dog of his took off. None of us could figure out what happened. He took the other dogs home and went out to look for the missing one."

She breathed a sigh of relief, not glad that the dog had been lost, but glad that her father hadn't been injured or worse. After seeing what had happened to Bill, her imagination had run wild with Dave's words.

She hurried the rest of the way to the pole barn and pulled open the door, not even pausing to look around as she reached for the phone. She dialed the emergency number and explained what had happened, agreeing to stay on the property and be ready to lead the emergency workers to the body.

By the time the dispatcher told her someone was on the way, Dave had joined her. He didn't say much, just stood there wringing his hands, his pale face full of concern. She didn't blame him. He, and her father, though he didn't yet know it, had just lost a friend.

It took longer than she had expected for the paramedics to arrive and for her to lead them back to where she had left Malcolm and Bill. Malcolm was still there, standing next to the body, shifting from foot to foot out of cold.

Angie watched as the men loaded Bill up after the pair of police officers that had followed them took photos of the scene. As they began the journey back to the house, all she could think of was her father and how he would respond when he learned what had happened. He had known Bill for longer than she had been alive. What would his friend's death do to him?

7

By the time she was done answering the questions for the police and had returned the snowmobile to Malcolm and retrieved her car, it was well into the afternoon. She called the diner to make sure everything was under control there, then decided to just go home.

She already knew that her mother would be waiting for her — Cheryl had arrived shortly before the police left, and had told Angie she had dropped her mother off at home. However, she was surprised by the tight hug and warm tea that were waiting for her.

"Oh, Angie, you must have had a horrible day," her mother said, taking a seat across the table from her. "Dave called Cheryl and told her what happened while we were in the car. I'm so sorry you got dragged into something like this."

"I wouldn't have been able to spend the rest of the day at the diner, not without knowing who the lost dogs belonged to. I was terrified that Dad was out there somewhere, hurt and alone."

"Oh, Angie." Her mother reached across the table and took her hand. "I'm so sorry. We should never have asked you to come up here. If you had stayed in California, you would never have had to deal with any of this."

"It's okay, Mom," she said. "None of us could have known something like this would happen. I'm glad I came back."

She gave the older woman a tight smile and patted her hand. She didn't want either of her parents to feel bad about asking her for help, no matter the fact that she had been daydreaming of California's beaches every time she stepped outside and saw the snow. What happened to Bill truly wasn't their fault, and she could have just as easily witnessed a gruesome accident back at her apartment.

"What we really have to focus on right now is how we're going to tell Dad."

With a stricken look on her face, her mother nodded. "It's going to break his heart. The two of them were practically brothers."

Angie's nerves only increased as the time passed by, afternoon inching into evening as she and her mother waited for her father to return. *I wonder if he's had any luck*, she thought. *The dog could be miles away. I'll help him look tomorrow if he doesn't find it tonight.*

When she finally spotted his truck, with the dog box in the back, pulling up the driveway, it just made her stomach twist even more violently on itself. The prospect of telling her father that his best friend, a man he had grown up with, gone to school with, shared a hobby with for years, had passed away made her want to run back to California and hide in her apartment more than anything else had.

She watched through the window as he parked the truck and opened the dog box in the back, lifting a dog — she couldn't tell which from this distance — into his arms and carrying it toward the house. Once she realized he was going to bring the dog inside, she jumped into action, dragging Petunia's dog bed out of her bedroom — the husky didn't use it much anyway, preferring the human bed — and into the living room, setting it up by the fireplace before getting a bowl of water from the kitchen. This had been their setup for injured dogs during her childhood, and she doubted it had changed much in the years since.

Her mother was there to open the door for her father, stepping back as he carried the wounded dog inside. He grunted his thanks when he saw the dog bed Angie had put in the living room, and lowered the dog down on to it. The dog wasn't one she recognized. He was mostly black, with tan eyebrows and a splotch of white on his chest and toes. There was a bandage covering most of one of his back legs.

"How is he doing?" Angie's mother asked softly.

"I had to take him to the vet. He managed to get tangled up in a fence out on a farm a few miles away. The vet thinks he'll be fine once he's healed up."

"Do you have any idea how the line broke? Did he not have a neck line on?"

"I could have sworn I hooked the neck line up, but

he took off as soon as the tug line snapped. I must have forgotten. It looked almost like the tug line was cut. It's possible that mice chewed through it out in the barn, I suppose."

"What's his name?" Angie asked, gently stroking the dog's head.

"This is Oracle," her father said. "One of Petunia's pups, actually. Bill and I bred him with one of his dogs a couple months ago. She's due any day now." He patted the dog's head, a proud look in his eyes, then stood up with a grunt and started toward the kitchen.

Angie and her mother exchanged a look. It was time to tell him.

Her father vanished into the bedroom after they gave him the news. Angie and her mother decided to leave him alone for a little while, and Angie started making dinner. None of them were hungry, but they still had to eat. It was an unhappy evening, and she couldn't help but hope that nothing else went wrong. Losing a family friend was bad enough. Surely the worst was over.

8

Angie didn't see her father the next morning before she left for the diner. Maybe that was for the best, since she didn't know what she could possibly say that would make things better for him. One thing she hadn't expected, but should have realized, was that Bill's death was the talk of the town... as was the fact that she had been one of the people who had found him.

All morning, she spent time trying to deflect questions about Bill's accident. It got to the point where she asked Betty — who had the morning shift that day — to take over in front while she worked solely in the kitchen. This worked well, until the older woman came into the kitchen with an apologetic look on her face.

"Someone out front is asking for you specifically," she said. "His name is Malcolm, and he said he wants to make sure you're doing all right."

"Can you send him back here?" Angie asked.

She figured it wouldn't hurt to talk to him. Since he had been there with her yesterday, he wouldn't pester her for details like everyone else was. He would understand what she was going through. She was touched at the thought that he had come to the diner just to see how she was faring. Even though it had been the last thing on her mind the day before, she wasn't blind to how attractive he was. He was definitely her type, and if he had gone to high school in town, she knew she would have remembered him. He must have moved there after she left.

"Sure thing. How's that breakfast burger coming along?"

"The order's just about ready," Angie said. "Hold on just a second, and I'll plate it."

It was the last order for the moment, which would give her time to talk to Malcolm as long as no one else came in in the next few minutes. She slid the still sizzling burger onto the toasted bun, then topped it with a fried egg, hash browns, and cheddar cheese. She placed the finished burger onto a plate that already had cottage cheese and fruit salad sides, and put the entire plate on the counter by the door just as it swung open and Betty, followed by Malcolm walked through.

"Thanks, dear," Betty said as she took the plate. "I'll let you know if anyone needs anything. And you, young man, don't you start pestering her about what happened."

"Yes, ma'am," Malcolm said. "I don't have any intention of bothering her at all."

Betty gave him an approving nod, then left with the plate. Angie shook her head.

"I've known her my whole life," she explained. "She can be a bit over protective."

"Don't worry about it. It's nice to have people who care about you," he said. He looked around the kitchen with interest for a moment before refocusing his attention on her. "I just stopped by to see how you were doing, and to apologize for dragging you out of the diner like that yesterday. Like I said, I was expecting to find your dad."

"It's fine," Angie said. "Of course, I wish things had turned out better, but I'm not upset that you came here and got my help. How do you know my dad, anyway? I never got a chance to ask you yesterday."

"Oh, he's helping me get into mushing," Malcolm said. "I know you probably get a lot of people like this up here, but I've always dreamed of owning sled dogs, and after my divorce, my ex-wife moved back to Alaska with the kids to be closer to her parents. If I wanted to be able to see my children, I didn't have much of a choice but to move here. I decided I might as well follow my own dreams while I'm at it. I started attending races and volunteering, and I met your father a couple times and we got to talking. Once we realized we lived about a mile apart on the same road, he decided to take me under his wing. It's been great, and I've learned a lot."

Angie blinked. Malcolm had not only been married, he had kids? He didn't look like he could be more than a couple years older than her at most, not past his mid-thirties. She had turned thirty-one last spring. Was she putting things off too long? She had always vaguely planned to get married and have kids, the whole nine yards, but had always pushed it off toward the future. Malcolm was a living reminder that a lot of people already had families by her age.

"That sounds like my dad," she said at last, realizing that she had been silent for just a bit too long. "He loves anything to do with dogs, always has, and has been obsessed with mushing for as long as I've been alive, if not longer. He's always thrilled when new people get into it. Do you have a team yet?"

He shook his head. "When I moved here, I stayed in an apartment for a while until I found the right house. I already had one dog, who I brought with me — a German shorthaired pointer named Izzy. I didn't want to get in over my head until I had a place with a proper yard. Dave, my neighbor, sold me two of his retired dogs, and your father was going to help me raise a couple of pups from a litter he and Bill were planning. I won't be racing the Iditarod any time soon, but I enjoy even just going out on the kick sled with the older dogs." He frowned. "Though after seeing what happened to Bill... I think I'm going to be taking a short break. I knew that it's possible to get injured, of course, but it's different seeing it with my own eyes."

"What happened to Bill... it isn't common," she said.

"Even if you're careful, even if you do everything right, sometimes bad stuff just... happens." She fell silent, thinking of her sister.

"Yeah."

Neither of them spoke for a long moment. Angie was saved from the awkwardness when the diner's phone rang. She gave Malcolm an apologetic look, then hurried to go answer it. She was surprised to hear her mom's voice on the other line.

"Angie?"

"It's me," she said. "Is everything all right, Mom?"

"No, it's not. Angie... the police just came and took your father away. I don't know what to do. They said they need to ask him questions about Bill's death. They said it looks like it was a homicide!"

9

Angie lowered the phone from her head and stared at it, as if it was the phone's fault that she was losing her mind. Because, surely, she was hearing things. It just wasn't possible that her father had been collected by the police for questioning about his best friend's death of all things. The police must have made some mistake. There was no way Bill had been murdered. It had just been some horrible accident... right?

"Are you still there?"

Her mother's voice was tinny and faint from the phone's ear piece. Angie pressed it back to her ear with a frown.

"I'm here," she said.

"What are we going to do? We have to help your father somehow. I'd go down to the police station myself, but I can't drive, and I don't want to tell Cheryl what happened. She's a dear friend, but you know how she blows things out of proportion."

"I'll come pick you up," Angie said. "I'll just have to leave the diner early. Theo's supposed to be here soon anyway, Betty will just have to manage on her own for a little bit. Get ready to go, all right, Mom? The police must have made a mistake. You and I both know there's no way Dad would want to hurt Bill."

She hung up and put the phone back in its cradle only to realize her hands were shaking. Malcolm was staring at her, his eyes wide. He had only heard half of the conversation, but she knew it had been enough for him to guess something about what was going on.

"Everything okay?" he asked.

She shook her head. "No. My dad's been arrested, or taken in for questioning, or *something*. I need to go. Sorry for cutting this short, and it was really nice of you to come make sure I'm okay, but I've got to pick up my mom and see if we can do anything for my dad."

"I understand. Go make sure everything's all right. And let me know if there's anything I can do, all right? I feel bad because I was the one who dragged you into this in the first place."

"Don't. I'm sure my dad would have been dragged into it either way. Bill was his best friend, everyone knows they were practically brothers. I'm mostly just worried about what this is going to do to him. Not only did he lose his best friend, but now he's being accused of killing him? It would be like a punch to the gut for anyone."

She grabbed her things, told Betty a quick version of what had happened with a promise to catch her up later, then hurried out to her car for the second time in as many days.

She and her mother pulled into the police station's parking lot an hour later. Neither of them had spoken much on the drive, and Angie's fingers ached with how tightly she had been gripping the steering wheel.

She shut off the engine and went around to the back

to get her mother's walker out, trying not to show her impatience as she waited for her mother to get out of the car and start walking toward the building. She wanted to be inside, *doing* something, not out here feeling useless.

Inside the small police station it was warm and comfortable. It was an older building, with none of the bullet proof glass and metal detectors that she had seen at police stations down in California. There was a young woman behind a desk who looked familiar in a vague sort of way. It wasn't until she looked up and met Angie's eyes that she realized who it was.

"Maggie?"

"Who — Ange?"

"Yeah, it's me. Your dad mentioned you worked here, but this is still a surprise. Wow, it's good to see you."

"It's good to see you too." She smiled. "I was going to call you, but I wanted to give you time to get settled in first." She blinked, as if just realizing where they were. "Why are you here, anyway? Not in town, but at the police station."

"My dad's here," Angie said.

"Oh. Oh!" Maggie turned in her swivel chair and picked up a phone, dialing an extension. "Dad? The Seavers are here. Okay, I'll tell them."

"What's going on?" Angie asked as her friend hung up the phone.

"He's just about done talking to your dad. He wants me to bring you back to interrogation room two. It'll probably be a few minutes before he's ready to talk to you. Do you or your mom want coffee or anything?"

"I'm fine."

"I'll have some water if that's all right," her mother said. "Did he want to talk to me too?"

"He didn't say he did. Do you want to take a seat out here? I'll get you your water."

Maggie got up from her seat and slipped through a door. By the time Angie's mother was settled in one of the hard-plastic chairs against the front wall, she had returned with a bottle of water and a napkin.

"Here you go. Come on, Angie. I'll bring you back."

Angie followed her old friend through the same door she had just come through with the water. "I'm a little bit confused," she admitted as they walked through the police station. "We just came here to see if there was anything we could do for my dad. Why does your dad want to talk to me?"

"He said he was planning on stopping by the diner to ask you some questions later today. I guess he decided to talk to you now since you're here anyway."

"Does he really think someone killed Bill?"

Maggie shot her a look out of the corner of her eye. "Ange, you ate dinner at my house at least twice a week when we were younger. You know my dad. Do you really think he would drag your father, someone he's known for twenty years, in for questioning if he wasn't sure?"

Angie sighed. "I just... I can't believe someone murdered Bill. I *know* it's not my dad, but that still means it's probably someone else I know. It feels unreal."

"I'm sorry." Her friend's face was filled with sympathy. "For what it's worth, I don't think your dad did it either. But I'm no detective. I'm sure my dad has a reason for believing what he does." She opened a door and gestured Angie inside. "Go ahead and wait in here. It shouldn't be too long. He sounded like he was almost done. And I know this isn't the best time, but call me, okay? I'd love to catch up somewhere other than inside a police station."

"I will," she promised. "Thanks, Maggie."

She stepped into the room and her friend shut the door behind her. She looked around. It wasn't anything special. The walls were white, and the floor was a sort of beige color. There was a two-way mirror on one of the walls and a camera in the corner. The center of the room boasted a table and two chairs, with a third chair sitting off in the corner. She took one of the chairs at the table and nervously drummed her fingers on the surface, regretting her decision to decline Maggie's offer of a drink. It would have been nice to have something to do with her hands.

She had been worried she would have to wait a long time, but only a few minutes passed before the door swung open again and Mr. O'Brien walked in. *Detective O'Brien here*, she thought. Angie gave him a tight smile as he took the seat across from her.

"Hey, Angie. How are you doing?" he asked.

"Worried, mostly," she admitted. "Detective, I know my dad didn't do it. He's a good guy, and he'd have no reason to kill his best friend."

He held up a hand. "We'll talk about your father later. Right now, I just want to hear from you. Have you remembered anything else about yesterday? Something that might have slipped your mind in the moment? I know my officers already asked you some questions, but nobody was treating the death like a homicide yesterday. Sometimes different details come to light when you learn that foul play was involved."

"I... I can't think of anything. I've never been questioned about a crime before, so I don't know if this is okay to ask or not, but how do you know he was murdered, and it wasn't just an unfortunate dog sledding accident?"

"My suspicions were raised due to the nature of the wound on his head. I can't tell you more than that." He leaned back in his chair and sighed. "I know it's a terrible situation all around."

"I just don't understand how anyone can think my dad would do something like that." Her throat felt tighter, and she took a deep breath, trying to control her emotions. She wanted to make amends with her parents, not see one of them carted off to jail.

"Were you aware that your father and Bill had a falling out just a few months ago?"

She blinked. "No. He didn't say anything about that."

"I know you've been out of town for a long time, Angie. Did you talk to your parents often?"

"I... I video chatted with them a few times a year. Called my mom a couple times a week just to talk, but my dad... it was pretty much just the video chats with him."

"Then I'm not surprised he didn't mention it. I only know about it because he spent a week stomping around the diner and I asked him what was wrong after the third time he splashed coffee out of my mug because he set it down too hard."

"What was the fight about?" she asked, trying to envision a scenario where her father and his best friend stopped talking.

"Dogs," the detective said simply. "According to your father, Bill borrowed one of his dogs to round out his team for a race in Canada, and when he brought the dog back, he told your father it had accidentally bred with another one of his dogs. Your father told me he doesn't believe it was an accident, because Bill had asked him only a couple months ago if they could do the breeding that year. Your father wanted to wait until next year to see how Bill's dog matured. She's pretty young if I remember, only about a year and a half old."

"So Bill borrowed one of my dad's dogs and bred it without permission?" Angie frowned. It was hard to wrap her head around, but she could see how something like that might lead to a fight between the two of them. They were both passionate about their dogs and the sport. "Wait, was the dog's name Oracle?"

"I don't remember," the detective admitted. "I didn't think anything of it at the time. I told your dad it wasn't worth losing a friendship over, and he should make amends and move on."

She frowned. "Well, if the dog that Bill bred without permission *was* Oracle, I think my dad took your advice. He mentioned something about a litter of puppies that's due soon, and I know Oracle is the sire and one of Bill's dogs is the dam. My dad didn't seem upset at all, he even had a home lined up for some of the puppies. He and Bill were going to give some to a guy my dad's mentoring."

"I'll ask him what the dog's name is when I go back to talk to him," O'Brien said. "Look, I appreciate that you want to clear your father's name, but we're getting a bit off track. I need you to walk me through yesterday again. Start from the moment you woke up, and go through the entire day. Don't leave anything out. Even the smallest things — something your dad said before he left the house, his reaction to Bill's death, or how the body was positioned when you saw it — could help. If your father *is* innocent, a clear and concise timeline will do nothing but help."

Angie sighed and closed her eyes, trying to remember every detail of the day before.

10

It was another couple of hours by the time they were done at the police station, but as far as Angie was concerned, it was all worth it because her father ended up coming home with them. He was still a suspect. She knew that the only reason Detective O'Brien let him go was because he didn't have enough evidence to legally keep him there. Still, it was a relief to have all three of them in the car as they drove home that evening.

The ride was awkward and silent. Her mother, exhausted, was dozing in the passenger seat, and her father was sitting in the back, fuming. Angie kept her eyes on the road, ready for the day — for the week — to be over.

"Well, here we are," she said as she turned off the

PATTI BENNING

engine, desperate to break the silence. "Home sweet home."

"I'll help your mother in. Will you go unlock the door, Angie?"

She did as she was told, blocking the cats from the doorway as her mother and father climbed the steps to the porch. Once they were all inside, the three of them gravitated to the living room where they sat in silence on the couch. After a few minutes, Angie couldn't take it anymore.

"I'm going to go make tea," she said. "Does anyone else want some?"

"I'll take a cup. Thanks, dear," her mother said.

She got up, only to halt in her tracks when her father said, "Angie, wait. I need to talk to you about something."

Finally, she thought. *I'm going to get some answers. Oh, my goodness, what if he really did do it?*

She turned around, trying not to show her trepidation. "What is it?"

"You don't need to go in to the diner tomorrow. I'm

going to spend the day there. I need to clear my head, and I always think best when I'm there."

She blinked. "Is that it?"

He nodded. "I'll take some tea too."

"All right." Disappointed, she headed toward the kitchen. It seemed that her family really hadn't changed at all in the years since she had left. Whenever anything bad happened, it was met with silence and distance, and it seemed the worse it was, the deeper the silence ran. She knew from experience that any questions she asked would just be deflected, any answers she wanted would have to be dug out slowly and painfully. In many ways, it was easier just to pretend everything was okay than to risk the resentment her father would show if she tried to actually talk to him about something important. *Business as usual in the Seaver family*, she thought with a sigh.

With an unexpected day off, Angie decided to keep a promise to an old friend. She called Maggie shortly after she woke up the next morning and made plans to get together after her friend's shift ended that afternoon. She spent the hours before their get-together shopping for the little odds and ends she needed to make her room feel like home.

When she got to the coffee shop, her friend was already there, seated at a table by the window with a steaming latte in front of her. Angie made a detour to the counter so she could order her own drink, then joined Maggie.

"Hey," her friend said. "How are things going?"

"Remember when my sister passed away?"

"Of course."

"About half as bad as that."

"Oh. I'm sorry. That's... still pretty bad. I'm sorry if my dad's making things harder for you guys."

Angie shook her head. "Don't worry about it. I know he's just doing his job. Plus, I wouldn't blame you for anything he did even if he was being a jerk." She nudged her friend. "Let's talk about something else. How long have you been back?"

"Since summer." Maggie sighed. "I felt like such a failure crawling back to my dad after the divorce. He told me Brian was no good. I should have listened to him. I mean, I'm glad I didn't, because I have Josh, but still... the whole thing was a mess."

"I can imagine. I'm really sorry for not being better at keeping in touch, Maggie. You deserved more than a couple emails a year. I didn't even know you'd gotten a divorce until your dad told me."

"That's not just your fault," her friend said. "I could have reached out more." She smiled. "Let's just put all of that behind us, okay? We both suck at being long distance friends, we admitted it, now let's pick things up where they left off."

"Sounds good to me," Angie said, returning the smile. "So, tell me about your kid. What does he like to do? How is he adjusting to being here? It's so weird that I've never met him, but he's been this huge part of your life."

Maggie laughed. "You'll like Josh. He's a good kid. He was having a tough time at his old school, so I don't think he minded moving too much. Loves his grandpa. I know he wants a dog, but I don't think we have time for one. I told him maybe a cat, if he keeps his grades up this semester."

"You're so lucky," Angie said. "I'd love to have kids

one day. But I think there are a few steps that have to come first." She chuckled.

"Well, did you leave someone behind when you moved here? Someone special?"

"Not really. There was this one guy… he and I dated for a while, and I used to think he might be the one, but it didn't work out. We were starting to talk again, but I moved back here before anything could ever come of that."

"I'm sorry."

Angie shrugged. "It's okay, really. I liked him, and we got along great most of the time, but there just wasn't… passion, I guess. He's someone I can see myself keeping in touch with, but I don't really see us getting married anymore."

"I know you haven't been here long, but is there anyone local who's caught your eye? My dad's a horrible gossip, and he knows *everyone*, so I could dish on anyone you're interested in."

She laughed. "I've been here literally three days, Mags. I don't move that fast. I mean, Malcolm seems nice and he's definitely my type, but dating is the last thing on my mind now. Really."

"Malcolm? That single dad?"

"Yeah. I was surprised to learn that he was divorced and has kids. He doesn't look it."

Maggie raised an eyebrow. "Do I?"

"No! I don't even know what I'm trying to say. He just... doesn't look like a dad."

Her friend laughed. "I know what you mean, I'm just messing with you. Yeah, he seems nice. I don't actually know much about him. My dad's brought his name up a couple of times. I think he's trying to subtly nudge me to start dating again."

"If you're interested in him, I'll consider him completely off limits, I promise," Angie said.

"No, no. Really, I'm not even close to being ready to date again. You go for it if you want to. How did you meet him, anyway?"

"He lives just down the road from my parents. Right next to Cheryl and Dave's property. He spotted Bill's dogs running loose and came to the diner looking for help."

"Oh, I didn't know he was involved with all of that. I wonder if my dad will end up dragging him in too."

"In for what? As a suspect, you mean?"

Maggie nodded. "I know he spoke to both of your neighbors already. I think the only reason *you* aren't a suspect is because you've been gone for so long. There's really no conceivable motive for why you would want to kill him. Plus, you've got a pretty good alibi if you were at the diner all morning. I know you found the body, which would normally put you right at the top of his list of suspects."

"Technically Malcolm's the one who found the body. He was leading the way and he's the one who spotted Bill and pulled off to the side."

Her friend frowned. "I see."

"What?"

"I don't know. I mean, it just seems kind of suspicious, doesn't it? He just happened to find Bill's dogs, then he also found the body. And I doubt he has an alibi, since he works from home?"

"How do you even know that? And I could have just as easily found the body. It was just chance that he was in the lead."

"I told you, my dad's been pushing me to date. I

think he thinks a divorced dad and a divorced mom would be the perfect match. Anyway, you're probably right. One thing I don't understand is why Malcolm came all the way out to the diner to look for help instead of just going out to search himself. It must have taken almost an hour to get from your road to the diner and back again, and that's a long time to wait if you think someone might be hurt."

"He said he didn't know the trails very well and was worried about getting lost."

"Then why was he in the lead?" Maggie asked.

Angie blinked. She didn't have an answer to that. Was it possible that Malcolm had only wanted someone to go with him so any suspicion the police had about him might be deflected?

11

After her lunch with Maggie, Angie drove back toward her house. She was paused at the stoplight in the center of town, deep in thought, when she saw a familiar face going into an antique shop. Cheryl, accompanied by a man she didn't recognize. If she wanted to know more about Malcolm, who better to ask than their shared neighbor?

She waited until the light turned green then pulled through the intersection and into a parallel parking spot next to the sidewalk. She hurried to cross the street and go into the store, worried that Cheryl would leave before she got there.

The interior of the store was dark and dusty. There didn't seem to be any particular organization; furniture was lined up haphazardly, with tables and cabinets full of smaller antiques interspersed throughout. It took Angie longer than she expected to find the other woman. When she finally rounded a corner and saw Cheryl looking at a tea set, she breathed a sigh of relief and gave a small cough to alert the other woman of her presence.

"Angie!" Cheryl jumped, almost dropping the teacup she was holding. "What are you doing here?"

"I saw you come in, and I wanted to talk to you," she admitted. "It'll be quick. I just need to ask you something about Malcolm."

"Oh, Mal. He's a sweetheart. I feel so bad for him, living all alone like he does."

"He does seem nice," Angie said. "I was just wondering; did he get along pretty well with Bill? He's the one who found the body, you see, and if they were close, I'd feel terrible for him." It wasn't exactly a lie. She knew how much Cheryl loved to talk, and she didn't want to give the older woman any reason to start spreading a rumor that Malcolm had something to do with Bill's death if he was innocent.

"I think they got along pretty well," Cheryl said. "I never really saw them interact much, come to think of it. I know your dad took him under his wing, but he never really had much of a reason to spend time with the other guys. I think he'll be just fine, dear, but if you want to bring him something nice, baked goods are always appreciated. A homemade pie can say a lot."

"Thanks," Angie said. "I think that's all I needed to know. Sorry for bothering you, I'll let you get back to your shopping now."

She turned to go just as a man rounded the corner, nearly running into her. "Be careful, Fred!" she heard Cheryl admonish from behind her. The man grunted an apology and sidestepped to let Angie slip by. She left the antique shop with a heavy heart. Nothing Cheryl had said had been enough to either clear Malcolm's name or convince her of his guilt. She knew her father was innocent, which meant that either Dave or Malcolm must have killed Bill. They were the only two other people who had been near the property that day, and if Detective O'Brien was right about Bill's death being a homicide, that meant the killer was someone she knew.

The thought of one of her parents' neighbors being a murderer stuck with her for the rest of the drive home. Her nerves were already frayed when she turned into the driveway to see an all-too familiar vehicle parked where she normally parked the van. Malcolm was there.

Fear for her parents coursed through her veins as she pulled the truck up next to his car and shut off the engine. She headed toward the porch, but changed directions when she heard voices coming from the barn where her father stored his dog sledding gear. His truck was backed up to the entrance and she saw pieces of wood loaded into the back.

"Dad?" she called out.

"In here!"

She stepped into the barn to find her father and Malcolm taking apart a wooden dog house. Petunia was curled up on a pile of blankets next to the wall. She wagged her tail when Angie came in but didn't bother getting up.

"What's going on?" she asked.

"Bill's wife asked me for help with his dogs," her father said. "I don't have room for all of them, so I asked Malcolm if he wants to take some. I'm letting him use the old dog houses."

"What are you going to do with them all?" she asked.

"I might keep a couple, the rest will go to other racers," he said. "Bill's wife doesn't think she's in a place emotionally where she can take care of them."

"It will be good practice for when I have more dogs of my own," Malcolm said. "I've never had outdoor dogs before. Your father's going to make sure I do everything right so they're comfortable and happy."

"I see." Angie fell silent, trying to keep an eye on Malcolm while at the same time trying not to seem like she was staring at him. Ever since Maggie had planted the idea in her head about him being the killer, she hadn't been able to let it go.

"I was going to see if Mal wanted to stay for dinner," her father said.

"I don't have to," the younger man said quickly. "I don't want to intrude. I'm sure your family wants time together alone."

"It's fine," Angie said. "I mean, I don't mind at all. I'd like to get to know you better." Realizing that he might take that the wrong way and assume she was flirting, she quickly added, "Since my dad's mentoring you, and all. We'll probably be seeing a lot of each other."

"Well, if you're sure you don't mind, I'd love to have dinner here," he said, giving her a hesitant smile.

"Should I go tell Mom? If you're going to be done out here soon, I can get dinner started."

"Thanks, Ange," her father said. "We'll probably be in in about twenty minutes."

Angie left the barn and headed toward the house. She felt flustered, and wasn't sure whether it was because she was about to eat dinner with someone who might be a killer or because she was about to eat dinner with a man she was attracted to and she really did *not* want their first dinner together to be with her parents.

12

Dinner didn't help matters at all. Malcolm was never anything but a gentleman during the meal, and it was obvious that he knew her parents well. She felt a bit of guilt at the thought that they had taken him under their wing since their own children had all but abandoned them. She felt caught off guard during the whole meal, and couldn't stop staring at the man, which her mother noticed, judging by the wink the older woman gave her when she got up to clear the table.

By the end of the meal, she was no closer to finding out whether he was guilty or innocent. She went to bed with turmoil in her heart, and woke up dreading the coming hours. She had only been back in Alaska for a few days, and each one had come with its own disaster. This morning she was due back in the diner, and she just didn't know if she had it in her to be a smiling face to the customers all morning.

She got her first surprise when she opened the diner's door at seven-thirty in the morning to find a stranger already in the kitchen. She was a young woman who looked like she was in her early twenties. She had blonde hair, which was pulled back into a ponytail, and wore thick-rimmed glasses. She turned when she heard the door opening and gave Angie a bright smile.

"Hi, I'm Grace. It's nice to meet you. Your dad's been talking about you all month, ever since he learned you were moving back. I feel like I practically know you already."

"Hey," Angie said. "I'd introduce myself, but from the sound of it I don't really need to. Feel free to just call me Angie. Theo keeps trying to call me Mrs. Seaver, which makes me feel like an old, married schoolteacher."

"Okay. Angie it is. So, how do you like it here? Is it just like you remembered? Are you used to the cold yet?"

"It's been... interesting," Angie said as she walked over to the sink to wash her hands. "And yes, pretty much everything is like I remembered. The coffee shop is new, but that's about it. I'll never get used to the cold, I've resigned myself to that."

"Would you rather cook or serve? I don't mind, I'm happy doing either."

"I don't mind either," she replied. The young woman seemed nice, but talked a mile a minute. It was still early enough that Angie felt partially asleep. "You got your wisdom teeth out, didn't you? I listened to your voicemail. How did that go?"

"It was terrible," Grace said, cheerfully seizing the topic. "Well, not the surgery itself, I don't really remember that, but the day after was the worst. My mouth still hurts, and I have painkillers, but they don't work as well as I thought..."

She continued talking. Angie let herself relax into the conversation, putting everything else that had happened over the past few days out of her mind. She still had a lot to think about, but right now all she had to do was focus on her job. It was easy enough to relax into the routines of the day and forget, just for a little bit, what was going on at home.

Angie stayed for a little while after her shift to make burgers for herself and her mother. Her father had told her that morning that he was going to go over to Dave's for a beer and some television after work, so it would just be the two of them for dinner.

She drove home, feeling almost peaceful despite everything that was on her mind. *It really is beautiful here*, she thought. *I shouldn't have stayed away for so long.* She thought about her brother for a moment, living on the east coast with a fiancé she had never met, and resolved to send him an email later that evening. His fallout with the family had been worse than hers, but even so she was sure he would want to know everything that had been going on here.

After getting home, she set up some TV tables in the living room for her and her mother and they ate together while watching the news. The cats begged for food just as badly as any dog, and Angie broke off pieces of her burger to give them.

"So, which is which?" she asked her mother, gesturing at the cats. "I should probably learn how to tell them apart."

"Checkers has the white spot between his ears.

Chess doesn't," her mother told her. "And don't feed them your food, Angie. You're teaching them bad manners. Look at them, they know you're an easy mark. You don't see them pawing at *my* plate."

"Sorry." She waved her hand in an attempt to shoo Checkers away. "I'm still surprised you have cats. You always refused to get one when we were growing up."

"I couldn't very well turn two bedraggled, freezing kittens away, now, could I?" The older woman gazed at the cats fondly. "Really, it's Cheryl who convinced me to keep them. She pointed out that I could use some company in the house. Your father's gone a lot, and with me being unsteady on my feet, it isn't really safe for me to bring one of the dogs in when I'm alone. They aren't always very careful, and I'd hate to think what would happen if I got knocked over while no one else is home."

"Well, I'm glad you have them," Angie said. "And I'm glad you have Cheryl. She seems like a good friend. Does she take you into town a lot?"

"A couple times a month, usually," she said. "I was actually surprised when she called me the other day, we had just gone out the day before you arrived. I guess she just really needed to go to the store and didn't want to go alone. Between you and me, I didn't really feel up to it, but she just sounded so desperate on the phone I had to agree to go with her."

"That's nice of you, but I'm sure she'd understand if you told her you weren't up to going out. Did I tell you I saw her yesterday? She was going antique shopping with someone." Angie frowned. "I think his name was Fred?"

"Fred? Oh, dear."

"What?"

Her mother looked around as if double checking that they were alone, then lowered her voice. "I know you aren't one for gossip, Angie, but you can't even tell your father what I'm about to tell you. Okay?"

Confused, Angie nodded. "I promise. Now tell me, what's going on?"

"Two years ago, Cheryl told me she had started to see someone. A nice man named Fred. Your father knows him, I think. He lives in the next town over and goes on the yearly hunting trip with the guys."

"She was seeing him? But... she's married."

"I know." Her mother nodded. "I didn't approve, and I told her as much. I thought she broke it off with him, but if you saw them together, she must have started seeing him again."

"You said he goes on Dad's yearly hunting trip." Angie frowned. "Bill must have known him too."

"I'm sure he did."

"Mom... what time did Cheryl pick you up?"

"A little bit before eleven, I think. We had only been in town for a little while before you called us."

"Dad's over there right now?" Her mother nodded. Angie took a deep breath. "Mom, does he know about the affair?"

"I don't think so, dear, but I suppose it's possible. I'm sure he would tell Dave if he did."

Angie fell silent, staring blankly at the TV. It had all come together, with nothing but a few unexpected words from her mother. She had been foolish to suspect Malcolm. No, it was clear as day. Bill must have learned about the affair and threatened to tell Dave unless Cheryl came clean. Cheryl must have killed him to keep him quiet. And her father was over there right now, completely unaware that he was spending time around the person who had killed his best friend.

13

Angie called the police, telling Officer O'Brien everything she had learned. She was speaking so quickly that her words got jumbled and she had to restart from the beginning more than once. He promised he would send someone out to question Cheryl, but that wasn't good enough for her. If her father knew about the affair – which was likely, since Bill must have known, and Bill would have told him – and if he told Cheryl what he knew, chances were, he would end up as her next victim.

"I'm going over there," she told her mother as soon as she hung up the phone.

"What's going on, Angie?"

"I think I know who killed Bill, and Dad's in trouble."

"Ange –"

"I just need to make sure he's okay, Mom. I can't lose him now. Not when I still have so much time to make up for."

"I could come with you..."

Angie was already shaking her head. "You should stay here. I don't want you to get hurt."

"You mean, I'm useless."

"No, of course you're not. But if something goes wrong, we need someone to tell the police what happened."

"You can't go alone, Angie. You're my daughter, I'm not just going to stand by when you go into danger. If you don't want to bring me, fine, but at least bring someone. Why don't you call Malcolm?"

She hesitated, but then nodded. "Fine, but if he doesn't answer, I'm still going. Dad has no idea how much danger he could be in." She didn't know if Cheryl would try something, but she had already killed one person. If she suspected that someone else knew about the affair, there was no telling what she might do.

She found Malcolm's number in her parents' Rolodex and dialed it. He answered after a few rings.

"Hello?"

"It's Angie Seaver," she said. "Are you free?"

"I can take a break. What's up?"

"I need you to meet me at Dave and Cheryl's house in a few minutes."

"Did something else happen?"

"Not yet. I'll explain everything when we get there."

She hung up the phone and looked over to her mother, who gave a satisfied nod. "Be careful, Angie."

"I will be," she promised.

She got into the van and started the engine, gunning it down the driveway faster than was safe. It wasn't far to the neighbor's house, but by the time she got there she felt as though she was about to burst from anxiety.

She pulled into the driveway only moments before Malcolm did the same. The two of them parked their cars next to her father's track and got out.

"What's going on?" Malcolm asked. "Not that I mind having an excuse to step away from my computer, but you sounded worried on the phone."

"Cheryl was having an affair with someone my dad and Bill knew, and I think he found out and confronted her and she killed him for it. I don't know if my dad's the type to bring it up, but if he does... I just can't take the risk that she'd hurt him."

Malcolm blinked. "That's a lot to take in. How sure are you?"

"Pretty sure. It's the only thing that makes sense. Unless you did it?"

"Of course not! Wait, did you really think that? Why on earth would I want to kill Bill?"

She shook her head. "I'll tell you later. Right now, we have to find my father."

She started hurrying toward the large barn on Dave's property, hoping to at least find some hint of where they had gone if they weren't in there. Malcolm called out to her and she turned around to give him a questioning look.

"There's smoke coming up from the chimney. Someone must be in the house. Let's just go check there."

"Good idea."

They walked side-by-side up to the house. Malcolm knocked on the door and Angie shuffled from foot to foot until it opened. Cheryl smiled out at them.

"Come on in, you two." She turned her head to call back into the house. "Rod, your daughter is here. Malcolm's here too."

Angie felt a rush of relief when she heard her father call something back. She couldn't make out what he said, but she knew his voice. He was safe.

"Dave has been building a new dog sled, and Rod is helping him," Cheryl explained. "Your father is hoping to get into sled building, I think. I hope your mother's got a room in the house she's willing to set aside for his new hobby. Everywhere I look it's dogs this, sleds that... I keep telling Dave, this isn't what I signed up for when I married him, but does he listen? No."

She kept chattering as she led them through the house to the living room, where Dave was waxing one of the long runners for a dog sled. Her father was sitting in an armchair, and looked up when they came into the room, giving Angie a puzzled look.

"Is everything all right at home?" he asked.

"It's fine," she said.

"Why are the two of you here, then?"

"Don't be rude, Rod," Cheryl said. "They are going to think they aren't welcome."

"Of course they're welcome, I was just wondering why they are here."

"We need to leave, Dad," Angie said.

"Is your mother okay?"

"Yes, she's fine."

"Then why do we have to go? What's going on?"

She took a deep breath. "Because I know who killed Bill, okay?"

She froze. As soon as the words left her mouth, she knew that she had made a mistake. Sometimes her father just frustrated her so much, and it was difficult to control her temper when he was being obstinate.

Cheryl gasped. "Dave! Dave, it really was Rod. The police were right."

"No," Angie said. This was all getting out of control. Why couldn't anything go as planned? "My dad didn't do it. Don't you dare try to throw him under the bus." She glared at the older woman.

"What are you talking about, Angie?" her father asked, standing up. "If you know who killed Bill, spill it. I'm sure Dave and Cheryl want to know too."

Angie fell silent. Why wouldn't her father just listen to her and leave with them? She looked at Cheryl again and her eyes narrowed. How dare she try to bring Angie's family into all of this? Using her mother as an alibi was bad enough, but then spending time around her father with this innocent act just made matters worse.

"Angie?" her father said. "You're acting very strange. What's going on?"

Malcolm stepped up next to her, placing a hand on her shoulder and gently guiding her back so that she was standing partially behind him, placing himself between her and Cheryl.

"Rod, we think someone in this room is the killer. The police are on their way. Right now, it's safest if we all just go our separate ways."

Angie's father took a step back, his eyes darting between Dave and Cheryl. "Are you saying that one of them –"

"It was Cheryl, Dad," Angie snapped. "She was having an affair, Bill found out, and she killed him when he confronted her about it."

The silence in the room was so thick that it made it hard to breathe. Everyone was looking at Cheryl, who had a hand clutched to her chest.

"You think I – I –" she sat down heavily in an armchair. "How could you say something like that? You've known me your whole life, Angie. How could you think I'm a *killer*?"

"It's the only thing that makes sense," Angie said softly. "Like Malcolm said, the police are on their way. I just want to get my dad out of here safely."

"Oh... I can't breathe.." Cheryl gasped, still clutching her chest.

"Enough," Dave said. "You're going to give her a heart attack. She didn't kill Bill. I did."

Whereas there had been silence when Angie accused Cheryl, not even a moment of quiet passed before Angie's father roared, "*What?*"

Dave raised his hands, looking terrified. And she didn't know whether it was at her father's reaction or at the admission he had just made.

"He... he found out I drugged his dogs before the race last month. It wasn't anything dangerous, just something to make them a little bit sleepy, to where they wouldn't want to run. I just wanted one win. One. So, I could pin it on the sled and start selling them for some extra cash. I was about to pass him on the trail a couple days ago when he made his dogs stop, blocking my way. He wanted to confront me alone, probably so you wouldn't get involved. I didn't even know what was going on. He just spun around and punched me. Then he told me if I ever messed with his dogs again, he would do a lot worse than that. You've got to believe me, I never planned on it. I just lost control. He turned around to get back on his sled and I grabbed a big stick from the side of the trail and hit him with it. It was heavier than I thought, covered in ice... He just dropped to the ground. I tried to make it look like an accident. I never meant to kill him. I wanted to give myself more time to hide the body, so when I met you back at the house, I sabotaged your team so you would have to go home instead of practicing."

"You sabotaged..." Her father trailed off, his eyes going wide. "You mean you cut the line? One of my dogs got lost and nearly got killed, because of you."

Angie had never seen her father so angry. She was glad when Malcolm stepped forward and gently pulled him back. She didn't want her father to do something that would make the murder accusation the police had laid on him stick.

She glanced at Cheryl and saw that the woman looked like she was in serious trouble. She hurried over to her, glaring at Dave on her way. She wasn't frightened anymore. He didn't look dangerous. He was wide-eyed and terrified, and when someone banged on the front door, he jumped almost a foot in the air.

"Police, open up."

EPILOGUE

"Here's two smiley-face waffles with extra whipped cream, two sides of hash browns, one egg sunny side up, and one scrambled with extra cheese." She put the plates down in front of the two eager children, then turned to their father. "And one very boring oatmeal with raisins and maple syrup."

The children laughed, and Malcolm scoffed at her jokingly. "I think you mean 'healthy,' not boring. I think I lost the ability to eat large amounts of sugar for breakfast sometime around the time I started needing coffee just to feel like a person in the morning."

Angie watched as Malcolm's children dug into their waffles. "Well, it doesn't seem to be genetic."

"Give them ten or fifteen years, you never know. Thanks, by the way. For the waffles. I wasn't sure where to take them."

"Hey, kids are always welcome at Lost Bay Burgers. My father and I are supposed to be switching weekends, but if you ever come in on a day when I'm not here, I'm sure you'll be able to convince him to do smiley faces on their food too."

"I brought them here once before you started working here," he told her, lowering his voice. "He stopped by the table to say hi, and the kids told me that the grumpy cook scared them. I was only able to convince them to come back by promising that he had been replaced by a pretty cook who is not scary at all."

Angie gave a snort of laughter that she tried to disguise as a cough. "I should head back into the kitchen before Betty hunts me down. Is there anything else I can get you?"

"I don't think so." He looked at his kids, who were busy eating. "I was wondering... how is your father doing? I haven't seen him for nearly a week."

"Well, his best friend is dead, his neighbor is looking

at a life sentence in prison for murder, and his dear daughter – that would be me – almost put his neighbor's wife in the hospital from a heart attack. He is probably going to spend another couple of weeks ignoring everyone before he is willing to talk about anything. Are you still watching Bill's dogs?"

"I am. I was expecting that they would have found new homes by now."

"Well, I can come out and help you with them if you want. It's not like you live far away. And I feel bad, since my dad is the one who roped you into all of this in the first place."

"If you do that, you should let me buy you a cup of coffee. Or even lunch, if you want." He hesitated. "It could be a date. Or not. Up to you."

She smiled. "Lunch, sometime this week?"

"Just name a day and a time, and the place, and I'll be there."

"It's a date."

ALSO BY PATTI BENNING

Papa Pacelli's Series

Darling Deli Series

AUTHOR'S NOTE

I'd love to hear your thoughts on my books, the storylines, and anything else that you'd like to comment on—reader feedback is very important to me. My contact information, along with some other helpful links, is listed below. If you'd like to be on my list of "folks to contact" with updates, release and sales notifications, etc.... just shoot me an email and let me know. Thanks for reading!

Also...

... if you're looking for more great reads, I am proud to announce that Summer Prescott Books publishes several popular series by Cozy authors Gretchen Allen and Patti Benning, as well as Carolyn Q. Hunter, Blair Merrin, Susie Gayle and more!

CONTACT SUMMER PRESCOTT
BOOKS PUBLISHING

Twitter: @summerprescott1

Blog and Book Catalog: http://summerprescottbooks.com

Email: summer.prescott.cozies@gmail.com

And...look up The Summer Prescott Fan Page and Summer Prescott Publishing Page on Facebook – let's be friends!

To download a free book, and sign up for our fun and exciting newsletter, which will give you opportunities to win prizes and swag, enter contests, and be the first to know about New Releases, click here: http://summerprescottbooks.com

42032097R00085

Made in the USA
Lexington, KY
12 June 2019